THE DINOSAURS NEXT DOOR

Harriet Castor

Designed by Maria Wheatley

Illustrated by Teri Gower

Edited by Emma Fischel

Language and Reading Consultant: David Wray
(Education Department, University of Exeter, England)

Series Editor: Gaby Waters

First published in 1994 by Usborne Publishing Ltd, Usborne House, 83-85 Saffron Hill, London EC1N 8RT, England. Copyright © 1994 Usborne Publishing Ltd.

Stan lived at number 3,
Green Street.

Mr. Puff lived
next door.

From the outside,
Mr. Puff's house
looked a little
strange.

Inside, it was even stranger...

Mr. Puff's house had rooms
full of very strange things.

Some were machines
that he had built.

4

Some were bits and pieces
that he had collected.

Some were things
that even Mr. Puff
couldn't explain.

Mr. Puff had a cat, too.
What was her name?

One day, Stan knocked
on Mr. Puff's door.
Mr. Puff opened it and said:

Hello, Stan.
There's something
I want you
to see.

Stan followed him inside.

Mr. Puff dived under the table.

He brought out a large basket.

Eggs?

Not just any old eggs. They're...

Dinosaur eggs. Handle with care.

But Stan already knew what they were. Do you?

Just then, one of the dinosaur eggs began to bump and jump.

Then a crack appeared...

and another...

until finally, a head popped out.

By lunchtime, all the eggs had hatched.

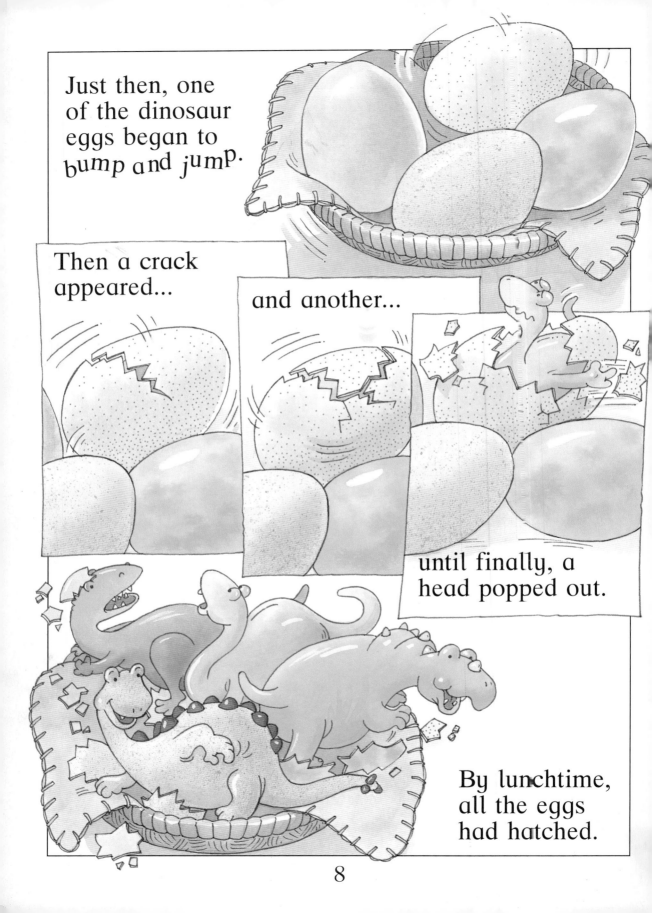

Mr. Puff fetched a book.

What did the book say dinosaurs ate?

Stan wasn't sure what sort of dinosaurs all these were.

He put out some salad and some cat food, just in case.

During the next three days, the dinosaurs grew...

and grew.

They're getting very fierce.

On the fourth day, Mr. Puff was worried.

Then he had an idea.

He rummaged in
one of the rooms
and dragged something out.

What was it called?

11

Mr. Puff gave Stan the hose
and told him to point it
at a dinosaur.

Then he pushed a lever.

There was a cloud
of starry smoke.

The dinosaur
had gone away.

Or had it?

Can you see where it has gone?

13

Stan and Mr. Puff
set to work on the
other dinosaurs.

One was in the garden.

Another was in the kitchen.

The last one was in the bathroom.

But just as Mr. Puff pushed the lever, the dinosaur lunged at Stan.

Slippo bath oil

Stan slipped, and the hose flew out of his hand.

What did Stan slip on?

The smoke cleared. Stan couldn't believe his eyes.

Everything around him was enormous... except Mr. Puff.

Eek! The Size-o machine has shrunk us as well as the dinosaur!

They heard a...

roar

Look at those teeth. Run!

16

Suddenly,
the dinosaur
turned its head.

What has the
dinosaur seen?

17

Amy chased the dinosaur away.

Clever cat!

Now we must use the Size-O machine to make us grow again.

First, they had to turn the dial.

It was hard work.

Then they moved the hose into place.

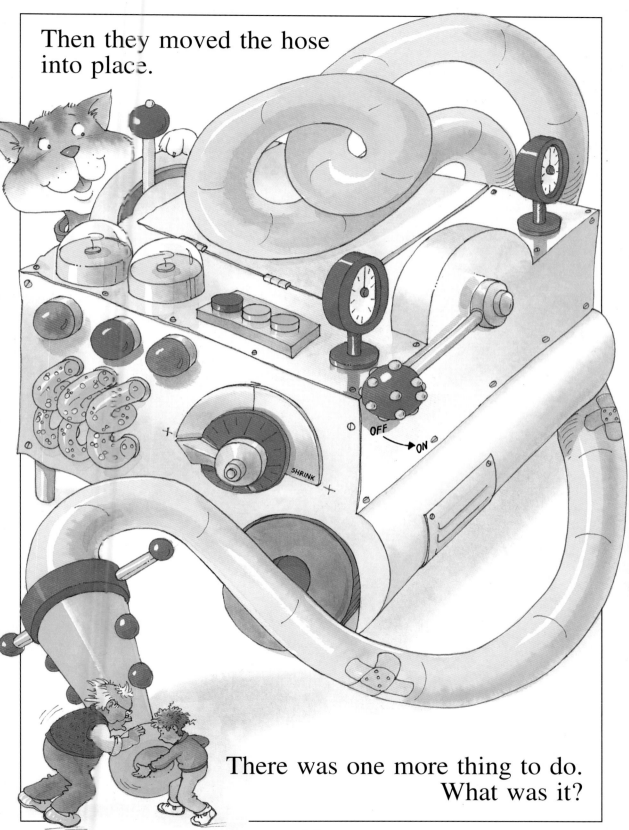

There was one more thing to do.
What was it?

The lever was high above them. Stan climbed onto Mr. Puff's shoulders.

OFF

SHRINK

But he couldn't shift it.

Then they both climbed up and bounced on the lever.

But that didn't
work either.

Just then,
Amy jumped up onto
the Size-O machine.

Down went the lever.

There was a
cloud of smoke.

At last Stan
and Mr. Puff
were back to
normal size.

22

Mr. Puff and Stan went
to find all the dinosaurs.

I think
they would make
nice pets.

Stan wasn't so sure.
In fact, he was quite
glad to go home.

Mr. Puff offered Stan
a dinosaur to take home.
But Stan chose
something else instead.

What was it?

Stan didn't tell anyone about the dinosaurs next door - or about his narrow escape.

You're a very clever cat.

But whenever he saw Amy, he always went out to give her a saucer of milk.